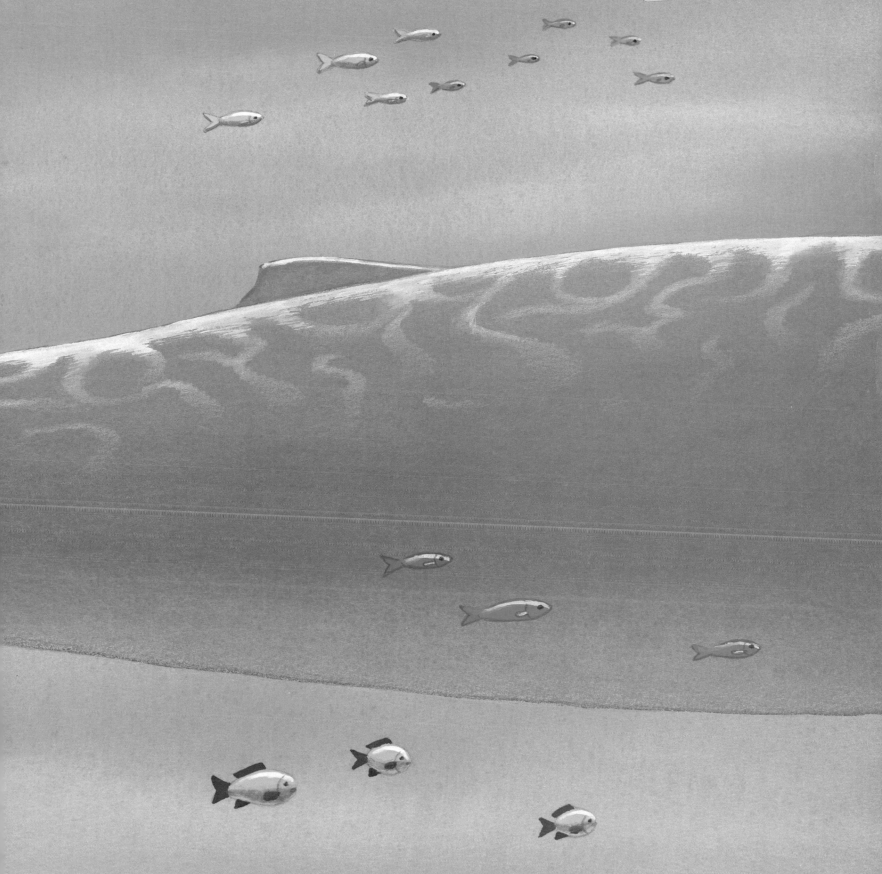

To my brother Alan

UNIVERSITY OF CHICHESTER

First published in Great Britain in 2008 by Bloomsbury Publishing Plc
36 Soho Square, London, WID 3QY

A CIP catalogue record of this book is available from the British Library

ISBN 978 0 7475 9254 9

Printed and bound in China

1 3 5 7 9 10 8 6 4 2

All papers used by Bloomsbury Publishing are natural, recyclable products
made from wood grown in well-managed forests. The manufacturing processes
conform to the environmental regulations of the country of origin.

www.bloomsbury.com

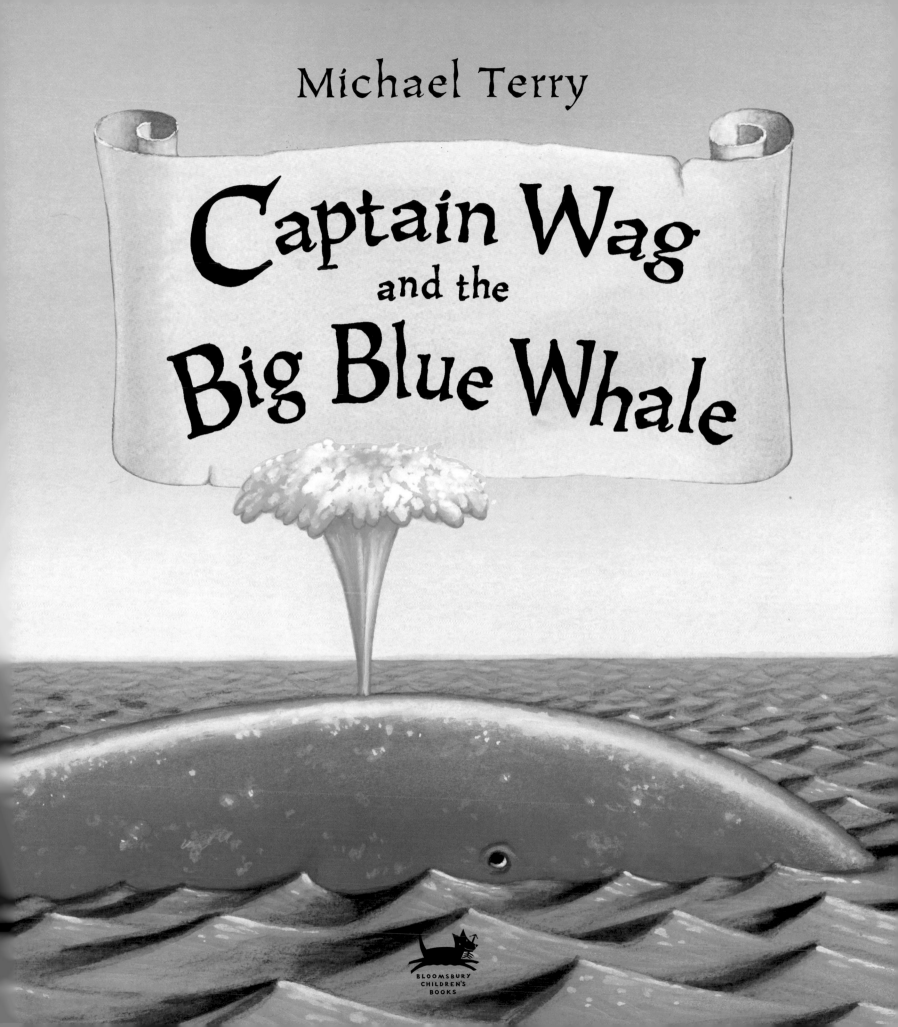

Michael Terry

Captain Wag
and the
Big Blue Whale

BLOOMSBURY
CHILDREN'S
BOOKS

Captain Wag and his trusty shipmates One-Eye Jack and Old Scratch have been marooned! Down to their last rations, they only have a few dog biscuits and bones in their treasure chest. They are very hungry . . .

'We've got to get off this pesky island, lads,' said Captain Wag.
  'How, cap'n? We haven't got a boat. That varmint Ginger Tom
took it,' exclaimed One-Eye Jack.
  Captain Wag thought carefully. 'Then we will have to build one,'
he said.

Captain Wag's two shipmates looked at him in wonder.
  'How are we going to do that, cap'n?' asked Old Scratch.
  'Look around, lads. There's plenty of driftwood and we can use branches from the palm trees. We've got all we need. Come on, let's build ourselves a boat and get home!'

Two days later, the three friends stood back to admire their work.

'She's a strange-looking vessel, shipmates, but I think she'll see us home,' said Captain Wag confidently.

They loaded the few biscuits and bones
they had left on to their boat, and
some coconuts, and set sail for home.

After many days at sea,
their supplies had run out.
They were starving and
thirsty and the boat was
starting to fall apart.

Suddenly, One-Eye Jack shouted, 'SHIP AHOY!'
  Captain Wag grabbed his telescope.
  'Aye, shipmates, it's a ship all right . . . but it's Pirate
Ginger Tom and he's coming this way!'

It wasn't long before Pirate Ginger Tom's ship drew
alongside Captain Wag and his sinking boat.
   'Well, well! Look what we've found, catmates — that old sea
dog Wag and his motley crew in a fine old vessel,' jeered
Pirate Ginger Tom.

'We could do with a few hands to clean the decks and wash the dishes. What do you think, me hearties?' cried Ginger Tom to his crew.

'You'll not take us on board your barnacle-ridden old ship, Ginger Tom,' shouted Captain Wag defiantly.

Pirate Ginger Tom just laughed. 'That's what you think,' he said.
'Get down there, lads, tie them up and bring them on board.'
But before his crew could reach Captain Wag's boat, a huge
shape slid beneath both vessels.

Suddenly, Captain Wag and his crew were lifted into the air. Pirate Ginger Tom's ship heeled over and nearly capsized!

'IT'S A SEA MONSTER!' cried Ginger Tom's crew in fright and they clung on to their ship for dear life.

As the sea washed away from beneath them, they could see what it was . . .

'It's not a sea monster, lads. IT'S A WHALE!' exclaimed Captain Wag in relief. And there they were, riding high on the back of a big blue whale and heading away from Pirate Ginger Tom and his motley cats.

Luckily for Wag and his crew, the whale swam on for the rest of the day before diving deep down under the waves. And as it did . . .

'Land ahoy, cap'n!' cried Old Scratch.

Captain Wag looked through his telescope and saw a familiar harbour and town ahead.

'Looks like we've struck lucky, lads. We're home, me hearties! We've escaped that Pirate Ginger Tom and his moth-eaten crew of cats!'

And Captain Wag, One-Eye Jack and Old Scratch laughed heartily and long as they finally made their way back home.

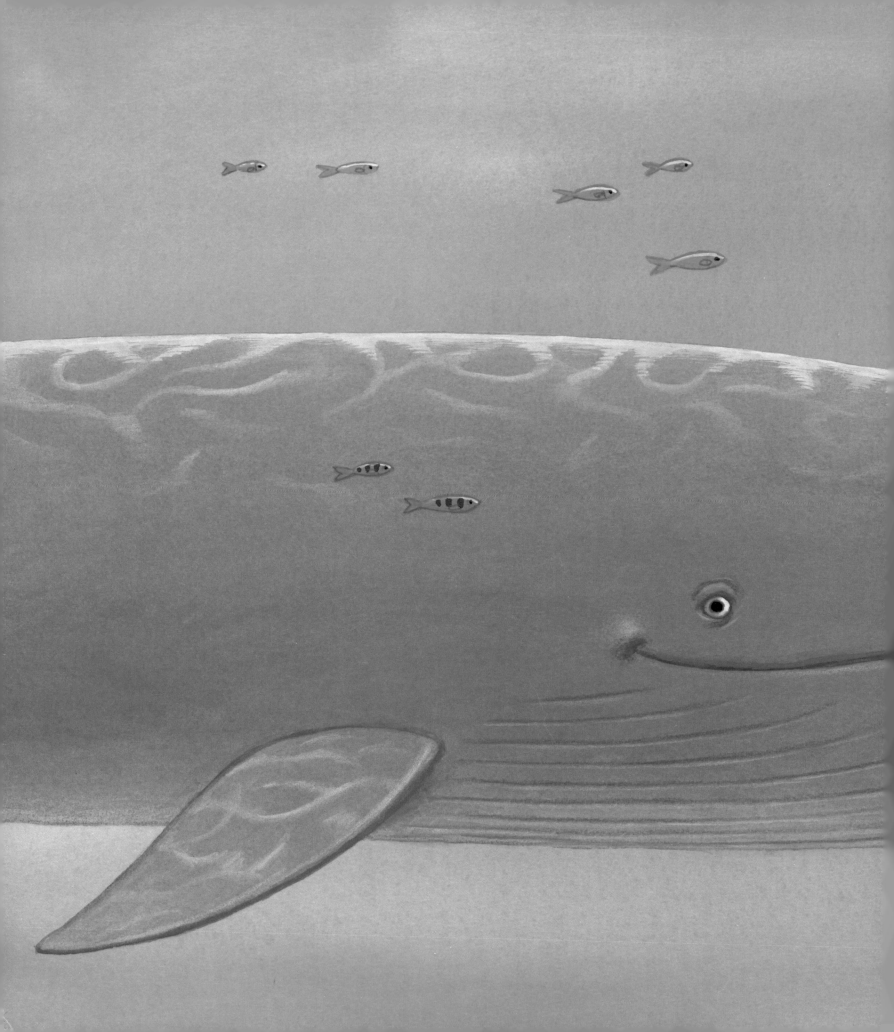